THE  ™

LEARN ABOUT SOCCER

with WOODIE SCORE, KATIE KICKER and FLOSSIE FOOT in

HIDDEN TALENTS

Sport Mites™ characters created and illustrated by Bob Pelkowski

Text by Rory Real

BARRON'S
New York ● London ● Toronto ● Sydney

ISBN 0-8120-4393-6
PRINTED IN HONG KONG

It was the last day of school. Katie Kicker and Flossie Foot sat listening to their teacher. The teacher was telling the class that their summer assignment was to discover their hidden talents. A hidden talent was something—anything—that they did especially well.

While walking home from school, the two girls talked about what their hidden talents might be.

"I am going to play the piano," Katie said. "My older brother takes piano lessons and so will I."

"I am going to sing," Flossie added. "My mother sings in our church choir and I will too."

Katie and Flossie said goodbye and each went home in search of her hidden talents.

When Katie got home, she went straight to the piano in the living room. She opened up one of her brother's music books and looked for a song to play. All of the pages had funny writing on them. Katie did not know how to read music so she decided to make up a song.

Katie first tried playing soft and slow. Then, she tried playing fast and loud. No matter what she tried to do, nothing sounded like a song. Katie decided playing the piano was not her hidden talent.

Over at Flossie's house, Flossie was practicing her singing. She tried to sing the same songs her mother sang in church, but for some reason they did not sound the same. Sometimes Flossie's voice would crack and other times it sounded like she was gargling. When Flossie tried to sing the high notes, nothing would come out of her mouth at all. Singing was not Flossie's hidden talent.

Both girls went over to the Sport Mites' clubhouse to think
about their talents.

"I don't play the piano very well," Katie admitted to Flossie.

"And I don't sing that well either," Flossie replied.

The girls sat with their chins in their hands and thought
about what they were good at.

Just then, their friend Woodie Score came running into the clubhouse. Woodie was very good at soccer and wanted to be a professional player when he grew up.

"Do you two want to play soccer?" he asked them.

"No, we can't play right now," Flossie told Woodie.

"We have to work on our hidden talents first," added Katie. The two girls sat quietly and thought again about what they were good at, as Woodie went back outside.

"Maybe we are good at painting pictures," Katie thought out loud.

"I don't think so," Flossie said. "It's too messy."

"How about cooking?" Katie questioned.

"No," Flossie said. "My mother won't let me use the oven."

The girls felt sad because they couldn't think of something—anything—that they were good at.

"I am tired of looking for my hidden talent," Katie mumbled. "It's time to have some fun. Let's go find Woodie and play soccer with him."

The girls found Woodie playing in the field behind the clubhouse. He and some of the other Sport Mites were getting ready to start a soccer game.

"Can we play on your team?" the girls asked Woodie.

"Sure," Woodie said. "We need two more players to even up the sides."

Everyone pitched in to help set up the playing field. Katie's and Flossie's job was to put up the goal nets at each end of the field. One net was for the Sport Mites and the other net was for the visiting team. Woodie's father came over to the field to be the referee. The referee is someone who watches the game and makes sure everybody follows the rules.

Woodie's father explained the rules to both teams. The object of the game was to get the ball into the other team's goal. But they could not use their hands. They could use their feet. They could use their knees. They could even use their heads. But only the goalkeepers could use their hands. The goalkeepers or goalies were the players on each team who stood in front of the goal and tried to stop the ball from going into it.

The two teams got ready for the opening kick-off. Each team decided which players would be forwards and which players would be defensemen. The forwards played upfield near the other team's goal and tried to kick the ball into the net. The defensemen stayed backfield by their own goal and tried to take the ball away from the other team. Katie and Flossie were both forwards; Woodie was the goalkeeper for the Sport Mites.

By the time the soccer game started, a couple of younger kids were sitting along the sidelines watching. Woodie's father whistled to start the game, and the two teams began running up and down the field. Each player tried to pass the ball to other players on his or her team until someone was able to kick the ball into the goal.

Katie could run and dribble the ball from one foot to the other. Flossie could bounce the ball off her knee and then kick it while it was still in the air. Both girls were having so much fun playing soccer, they did not notice that some parents and neighbors had come out to watch them play.

Everytime someone on the visiting team would score a goal, Flossie or Katie would come right back and score a goal for the Sport Mites. After a while the score was tied six to six. Katie and Flossie had each scored three goals. Redbert, the Sport Mites' mascot, kept track of the goals by writing the score on a large piece of wood for everyone to see.

SOCCER SCORE

PERIOD 1   PERIOD 2

SPORT MITES   3   3

VISITORS   3   3

After two periods of play, regulation time was up. Woodie's father made an announcement.

"The score is tied and time has run out," he said. "We will play a sudden death period where the next team to score a goal wins the game."

All the kids cheered with excitement.

The visiting team won the coin toss, so they kicked off to start the sudden death period. One of their forwards took a very hard shot at the Sport Mites' goal. Woodie jumped very high and caught the ball just before it went in. Woodie was the goalie, so it was alright for him to use his hands.

Woodie raised the ball over his head and threw it downfield as far as he could. The ball went to Katie. Katie started running toward the visitors' goal, pushing the ball ahead of her with her feet. Then, she passed the ball to Flossie.

But the ball never made it to Flossie. A player on the other team used his hands to catch the ball while he was in the penalty area in front of his team's goal.

Woodie's father whistled to stop the game. "That was a penalty," he said. "That means the Sport Mites get to take a penalty kick."

Woodie's father placed the ball in the penalty area directly in front of the visitors' goal.

"Who is going to take the penalty kick?" he asked.

All the Sport Mites huddled up to decide who would kick the ball. Katie and Flossie had both scored goals for their team. Everyone agreed that it should be one of them. But no one could choose between them.

"Let's toss a coin," Woodie shouted as he reached in his pocket for a quarter. "If it's heads, Katie will kick the penalty shot; if it's tails, Flossie will kick it," he explained.

Then, Woodie threw the quarter high into the air and watched it land near his feet.

"Tails!" the Sport Mites yelled.
"Flossie will kick the ball," Woodie told the referee.

Flossie went to the ball that was placed in the penalty area. The visiting goalkeeper took her position on the center of the goal line. She was not allowed to move until the ball was kicked. All the other players from both teams stood behind Flossie and watched her closely. The people along the sidelines watched closely, too.

Flossie took a deep breath and looked all around. She saw her parents and Katie's parents watching from the sidelines. She closed her eyes and thought about where she was going to kick the ball. She pictured the ball going into the lower left-hand corner of the net.

Flossie opened her eyes and took another deep breath. Then she ran up and kicked the ball as hard as she could.

The visitor's goalie dove for the ball, but it went right past her. Flossie had scored the winning goal! Katie, Woodie, and the rest of the Sport Mites jumped for joy. The people watching joined in the excitement. They were clapping their hands and shouting, ''Good game! Good game!''

As the Sport Mites went back to the clubhouse, all of their mothers and fathers told them how well they had played.

"You were great," Katie's mother said as Katie ran to her.

"Good game!" Flossie's father said as he gave Flossie a big hug.

Then, Woodie's father came over and shook Katie's and Flossie's hands.

"You are both very talented soccer players," he told the girls.

Katie and Flossie looked at each other and smiled. They had just discovered their hidden talents.

SOCCER EQUIPMENT

SOCCER BALL

SOCCER SHOES

SOCCER JERSEY
(long or short sleeves)

SOCCER SOCKS
(knee length)

SHIN OR ANKLE GUARDS
(worn under soccer socks)

SOCCER SHORTS

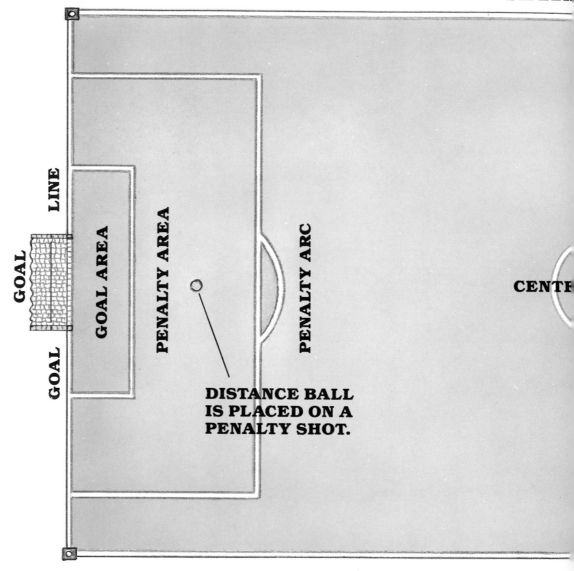

SOCCER FIE

SIDELI

CORNER MARKER

LINE

GOAL

GOAL

GOAL AREA

PENALTY AREA

PENALTY ARC

CENTE

DISTANCE BALL
IS PLACED ON A
PENALTY SHOT.

AGRAM

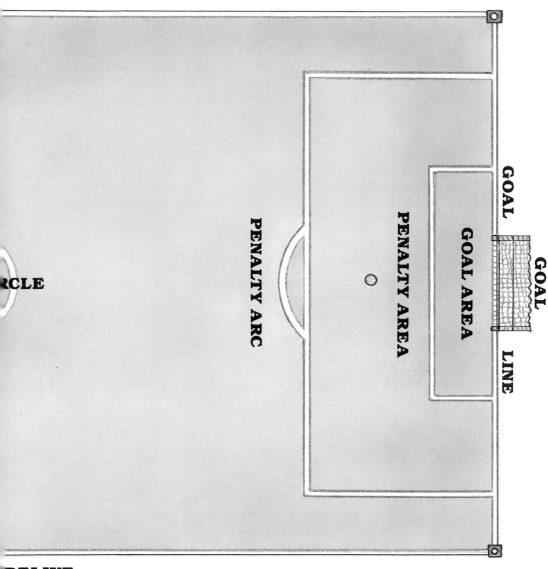

RCLE

PENALTY ARC

PENALTY AREA

GOAL AREA

GOAL

GOAL

LINE

DELINE

CORNER MARKER

SOCCER TERMS

defensemen   The players who guard the area by their own goal and try to take the ball away from any player on the other team who is trying to score a goal.

dribble   A method of moving the ball forward by kicking (passing) it from one foot to another while moving down the field.

forwards   The players who play upfield near the other team's goal and try to score a goal by kicking the ball into the goal or hitting it into the goal with their heads.

goalkeeper (or goalie)   The player on each team who stands in front of the goal and tries to stop the ball from going in. The goalkeeper is the only player on the team who can use his or her hands to catch or throw the ball.

goal   A large, box-like frame covered with netting on the back and sides into which teams must get the ball in order to score points.

kick-off   After a coin flip to see which team gets the ball, the referee places the ball on the ground and one of the players on the team that won the toss kicks the ball to a teammate to start the game. The ball must make at least a one-circumference turn before it can be touched by anyone else.

penalty   When a player does not follow a rule, the referee calls a penalty.

penalty kick   A player is given one chance to stand with the ball placed in front of the other team's goal and kick the ball into the goal with only the goalkeeper trying to stop it.

referee   Someone who watches the game action and all the players and makes sure everyone follows the rules of the game.

soccer   A sport played with two teams. Each team tries to get the ball into the other team's goal by kicking it or hitting it with their heads without using their hands, shoulders, or arms.

sudden death period   When the score is tied at the end of regulation time, the game is continued until one of the teams scores a goal to win the game.